If your child struggles with a word, you can encourage "sounding it out," but keep in mind that not all words can be sounded out. Your child might pick up clues about a word from the picture, other words in the sentence, or any rhyming patterns. If your child struggles with a word for more than five seconds, it is usually best to simply say the word.

Most of all, remember to praise your child's efforts and keep the reading fun. After you have finished the book, ask a few questions and discuss what you have read together. Rereading this book multiple times may also be helpful for your child.

Try to keep the tips above in mind as you read together, but don't worry about doing everything right. Simply sharing the enjoyment of reading together will increase your child's reading skills and help to start your child off on a lifetime of reading enjoyment!

The Emperor's New Clothes
A We Both Read® Book

Level 1

Text Copyright © 1997, 2014 Treasure Bay, Inc.
Illustrations Copyright © 1997, 2014 Toni Goffe

We Both Read® is a trademark of Treasure Bay, Inc.

Published by
Treasure Bay, Inc.
P.O. Box 119
Novato, CA 94948 USA

Printed in Singapore

Library of Congress Control Number: 97-62026

Hardcover ISBN: 978-1-60115-269-5
Paperback ISBN: 978-1-60115-270-1

We Both Read® Books
Patent No. 5,957,693

Second Edition

Visit us online at:
www.webothread.com

PR-11-13

WE BOTH READ®

The Emperor's New Clothes

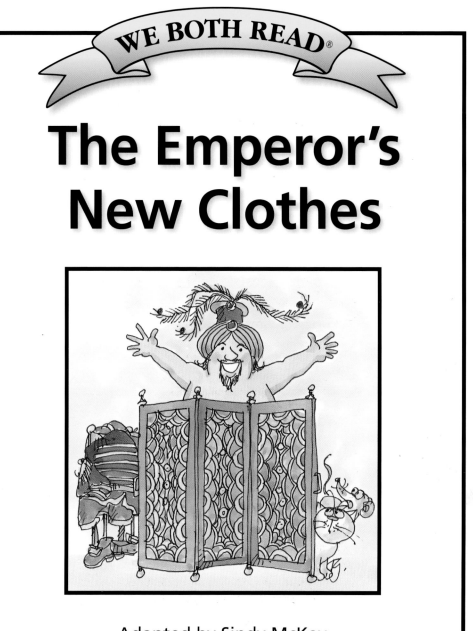

Adapted by Sindy McKay

from the story by Hans Christian Andersen

Illustrated by Toni Goffe

TREASURE BAY

Once upon a time there lived an emperor. He was a rich emperor. He was a handsome emperor. But most of all, he was a well-dressed emperor.

The emperor loved to parade through town, showing off his **fine** and fancy clothes. He would wave to the townspeople and say, . . .

"I like **fine** new pants.
I like them. I do.
I like fine new hats
and new socks and new shoes!"

3

One day, two strangers came to town, claiming to be weavers of a fabulous golden cloth.

"Our golden cloth has a magical quality," said the first.

"Some people **cannot** even see it!" said the second. The emperor was surprised by this.

4

"Some **cannot** see it?
Now how can that be?
Who cannot see it?
I hope it's not me."

The weavers assured the emperor he would see the magical golden cloth because he was clearly a wise emperor and the cloth was invisible only to a **fool**.

This gave the emperor an idea. He could use this magical cloth to learn who in his town was a **fool**! So he said to the weavers, . . .

"You will make it for me.
I must see what you do.
I will pay you with gold.
You will show me a **fool**."

The emperor gave the weavers chests full of gold. Then he sent them off to make their magical cloth, telling them, "**Don't** work on anything else."

As he waited for the cloth to be done, the emperor thought to himself, . . .

"I want to go see it.
I have to! I do!
But if I **don't** see it,
then am I a fool?"

9

So the emperor sent his faithful servant Fred to check on the progress of the **cloth**. When Fred arrived, the weavers showed him the weaving loom and told him they were weaving the magical **cloth** with threads of golden silk.

Fred, however, saw **nothing** at all. As he looked, he thought to himself, . . .

"Oh, no! I see **nothing**.
No **cloth** do I see.
But I will not say so.
No fool will I be!"

Fred rushed back and told the emperor of the wondrous beauty of the golden cloth. Excited by the news, the emperor gave the weavers more gold and told them to weave the cloth faster.

The next day, as he waited for the cloth to be finished, the emperor thought, . . .

"I'm sure I will see it.
I'll see it, like Fred!
I will go and see it,
but first—I'll send Ted!"

So Ted, another faithful servant, was sent to check on the progress of the cloth. The weavers told Ted that surely a man as wise as he could see that the cloth was now almost completed.

Ted, however, saw nothing at all. As he looked, he thought to himself, . . .

"I really see nothing.
No cloth do I see.
But I will not say so.
No fool will I be!"

15

Ted hurried back and told the emperor of the splendor of the golden cloth. So excited was the emperor that he paid the weavers even more gold to finish weaving the cloth the very next day!

The next morning the emperor woke up bright and early.

"It is time for a look.
It's a thing I must do.
I know I will see it
for I am no fool."

The emperor, with four faithful servants, set out to see the cloth. The weavers pointed to the loom and smiled. The weavers said that surely men as wise as the emperor and his servants **would** be able to see the finished cloth in all its glory.

The emperor and his servants, however, saw nothing at all.

They saw there was nothing.
No cloth did they see.
But they would not say so.
No fool **would** they be!

Each trusted servant praised the beauty of the cloth he did not see.

"It's brilliant!" said the first.

"It's amazing!" said the second.

"It's dazzling!" said the third.

"It's stunning!" said the fourth.

And the emperor eagerly agreed with their descriptions.

"I so love the cloth!
Here is what you must do.
You must make me some pants
and a fine jacket too!"

So the weavers began making the emperor a very special **outfit**. Taking the magic cloth from the loom, they pretended to cut it and stitch it with needles that held no thread.

Then they sent for the emperor.

"Come back now and see it.
The **outfit** is done.
No other is like it.
There is only one."

The emperor rushed back to see the weavers holding up their empty arms, as if displaying the emperor's new clothes. They bragged about the elegant pants and gushed over the long, flowing cape. The emperor appeared to be seeing it all.

"Oh look! There it is!
My new outfit is done!
I love it so much!
Now I must try it on!"

The weavers pretended to dress the emperor in his fine new outfit. As they pretended to place a cape on his shoulders, they remarked that it was as light as a feather. The emperor was delighted.

"I love how it feels!
It's like nothing at all!
This cape is so soft!
And it makes me look tall!"

Then the emperor turned to his trusted servants and asked what they thought. Since none of these men wished to be thought a fool, none would admit that he could not see the emperor's new clothes.

Instead they lavished praise on the clothes they did not see.

"I love how it looks."
"And the color is bold."
"The jacket fits well."
"And you look good in gold."

29

The next day the emperor paraded through town as he had so **often** before. He was not only excited to show off his new clothes but also to learn who in his town was a fool.

As he strutted down the street, a **crowd** began to gather.

" Just look at the **crowd**!
How they love what they see!
They don't **often** get
to see so much of me!"

Never before had so many **people** come out to see the emperor's new clothes.

And since no one in town wanted to be thought a fool, no one would admit there were no clothes to be seen.

"He looks good in gold,"
people said with a grin.
"And see how those pants
help to make him look thin."

Then, at last, a tiny voice spoke up from the crowd. It was the voice of a child. It was the voice of truth.

"I do not see pants
or a cape made of gold.
He better get dressed
or he may catch a cold!"

35

The townspeople could hardly believe their ears. Did that foolish child think the emperor was parading through town in his **underwear**?

The child pointed to the emperor.

"You say he is dressed,
and yet nothing is there.
He has nothing on
but his blue **underwear**."

Then another small voice spoke up, agreeing with the child about the emperor's clothes. Then another. And another. The small voices swelled. Then big voices joined in until finally the whole town spoke the truth.

"We do not see clothes,
just a belly that's bare.
We do not see clothes
because no clothes are there."

Soon everyone was seeing what was really there—and what was not.

As laughter began to fill the air, the emperor blushed and hid behind a bush. He had set out to discover who in his **town** was a fool, and now he knew.

"I looked for a fool.
Now at last I can see.
I found the **town** fool.
And the town fool is—*me*."

If you liked **The Emperor's New Clothes,** here are some other
We Both Read® books you are sure to enjoy!

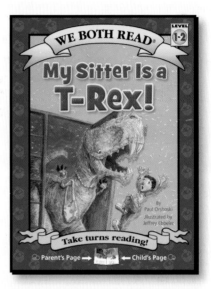

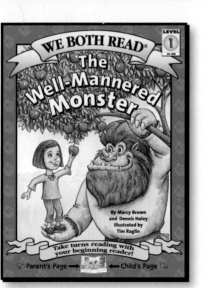